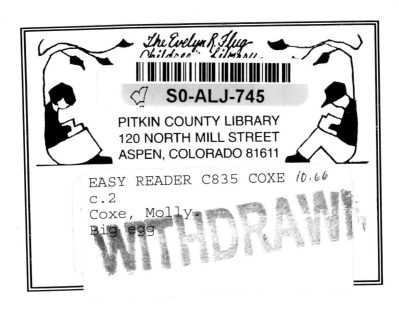

A NOTE TO PARENTS

Early Step into Reading Books are designed for preschoolers and kindergartners who are just getting ready to read. The words are easy, the type is big, and the stories are packed with rhyme, rhythm, and repetition.

We suggest that you read this book to your child the first few times, pointing to each word as you go. Soon your child will start saying the words with you. And before long, he or she will try to read the story alone. Don't be surprised if your child uses the pictures to figure out the text—that's what they're there for! The important thing is to develop your child's confidence—and to show your child that reading is fun.

When your child is ready to move on, try the rest of the steps in our Step into Reading series. **Step 1 Books** (preschool–grade 1) feature the same easy-to-read type as the Early Step into Reading Books, but with more words per page. **Step 2 Books** (grades 1–3) are both longer and slightly more difficult, while **Step 3 Books** (grades 2–3) introduce readers to paragraphs and fully developed plot lines. **Step 4 Books** (grades 2–4) offer exciting nonfiction for the increasingly independent reader.

The grade levels assigned to the five steps are intended only as guides. Some children move through all five steps very rapidly; others climb the steps over a period of several years. Either way, these books will help your child "step into reading" in style!

For Gee Gee

Library of Congress Cataloging-in-Publication Data
Coxe, Molly. Big egg / by Molly Coxe.
p. cm. — (Early Step into reading) SUMMARY: A mother hen wakes up one morning to find a gigantic egg among the others in her nest and goes in search of the egg's origin.
ISBN: 0-679-88126-3 (pbk.) — ISBN: 0-679-98126-8 (lib. bdg.) [1. Chickens—Fiction. 2. Ostriches—Fiction. 3. Animals—Infancy—Fiction. 4. Domestic animals—Fiction.]
I. Title. II. Series. PZ7.C839424Bi 1997 [E]—dc20 96-31978

Printed in the United States of America 10 9 8 7 6 5 4 3 2 1

STEP INTO READING is a registered trademark of Random House, Inc.

Early Step into Reading™

Big Egg

by Molly Coxe

Random House New York

Hen has some eggs.

One is big.

The rest are small.

"This is not my egg!"
says Hen.

"Is it a cat egg?"

"No," says Cat.

"Is it a dog egg?"

"No," says Dog.

"Is it a pig egg?"

"No," says Pig.

"Is it a cow egg?"

"No," says Cow.

17

"Is it a goat egg?"

"No," says Goat.

"Is it a fox egg?"

"YES!" says Fox.

21

The small eggs crack.

"Peep! Peep!"

say the small chicks.

23

The big egg cracks.

"SQUAWK!"

says the big chick.

"Run!" says Hen.

Hen has some chicks.

One is big.

The rest are small.

Hen loves them all.